Paddington

MICHAEL BOND

at the Fair

Illustrated by R.W. Alley

Collins

An Imprint of HarperCollins*Publishers*

One day in summer the Browns went on an outing to a part of London called Hampstead, where there was a big fair.

Paddington had never been to a fair before and he was most excited.

Mr Brown gave Jonathan, Judy and Paddington a pound each. "I should make the most of it," he said. "The fair only happens once a year."

First of all, Paddington had
a go on the Coconut Shy.
He hit the man in
charge by mistake.

"That isn't a very good start," said Mrs
Brown.

"Perhaps you should stand on something,"
suggested Judy.

Paddington thought that was a very good idea, and stood on his brown suitcase. After two more goes he had won a china bird for his bedroom wall and a picture of a goldfish.

"I shall call the goldfish Hampstead," he said, "after the fair."

And he gave his prizes to Mrs Bird to hold so that he could have a ride on the carousel.

Paddington enjoyed the carousel so much he went on it a second time.

"I think it's a very good way of travelling if you don't want to go anywhere," he called as he went past. "Especially if you have plenty of marmalade sandwiches to keep you going."

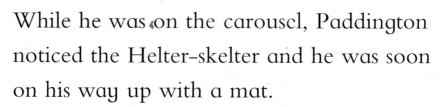

While he was on the carousel, Paddington noticed the Helter-skelter and he was soon on his way up with a mat.

"Did you enjoy that?" asked Mr Brown.

"Yes, thank you very much," said Paddington. "But it was a very quick way of spending fifty pence."

"That's funny," said Mrs Brown, looking up. "None of the other children are coming down. They all seem to be stuck."

"Oh, dear," said Paddington. "I think they may be sitting on one of my marmalade sandwiches."

"Perhaps we'd better go on the Space Craft before they find out," said Jonathan hastily.

Paddington liked anything new and he quickly climbed into an empty car.

He soon wished he hadn't. One moment they were climbing slowly up towards the sky. The next moment they came shooting back down again at breakneck speed.

SPACE
CRAFT

The cars went up and down and round and round. There were times when it felt as if they were going upside down as well.

"I wish I had chosen a different car," he groaned as they climbed out. "Mine felt as if it was trying to throw me out."

"I think they all felt the same," said Judy.

"Perhaps you should ask for your money back," joked Mr Brown, as he helped Paddington to his feet.

"I may ask for my stomach back," said Paddington darkly.

"How about trying something a bit quieter for a change?" said Mrs Brown.

"I don't think you'll find those very quiet!" called Jonathan.

But he was too late. Paddington was
already climbing into a Dodgem car.

He soon found out why some people
call them 'Bumper cars'.

By the time Paddington came off the
Dodgem cars it was getting late and he
had spent nearly all his money.

Just then he saw a tent with a notice
outside which said:

"Perhaps she will tell me where my next
pound coin is coming from," he said, and
before the Browns could stop him he had
gone inside.

Madame Grant looked at Paddington, then
she looked into her crystal ball. Then she
looked at Paddington again.

It was very hot inside the tent and
Paddington had his eyes closed.

"I think," she said, "I see a bear who
is going to sleep very well tonight."

And she was quite right. Paddington slept very well that night. In fact he slept so well he didn't fall out of bed once; not even when he dreamed he was back on the Space Craft.

Hampstead Fish

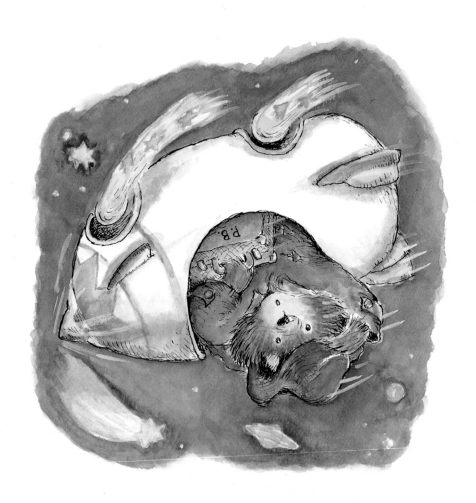